This Twinkl Originals book belongs to:

_____

_____

Listen and follow...

1 Scan the QR code using the camera on your phone or tablet. (You might need to download a QR reader first.)

2 Click on the link that pops up.

3 Press play to hear the story being read aloud.

4 Turn the page when you hear the twinkle!

First published 2020 © Twinkl Ltd of Wards Exchange,
197 Ecclesall Road, Sheffield S11 8HW

ISBN: 978-1-914331-25-1

FSC
www.fsc.org
MIX
Paper from
responsible sources
FSC® C022913

We're passionate about giving our children a sustainable future, which is why this book is made from Forest Stewardship Council® certified paper. Learn how our Twinkl Green policy gives the planet a helping hand at www.twinkl.com/twinkl-green.

Printed in the United Kingdom.

10 9 8 7 6 5 4 3 2 1

A catalogue record for this book is available from the British Library.

Twinkl is a registered trademark of Twinkl Ltd.

A Twinkl Original

Doris the Loris

Twinkl Educational Publishing

Doris the loris was a storyteller. From true stories to adventure stories and silly stories to love stories, Doris had a story for everyone.

Every evening, Cam the cuckoo sang to announce that storytime was about to begin. Creatures from all around came to Doris's tree and waited for her words to spark their imaginations.

Late one afternoon, Putu the pangolin was on his way to storytime. He spotted Gita the gibbon up in the trees.

"Why don't you join us for a story, Gita?" Putu asked. "Doris will sweep you away on adventures that you've never dreamed of!"

"I've told you before: swinging is all the adventure I need," said Gita. "Stories are boring."

"I will change your mind one day!" said Putu as he trotted off.

Doris told an exciting tale of a tiger who had bravely rescued its friend from a rushing river.

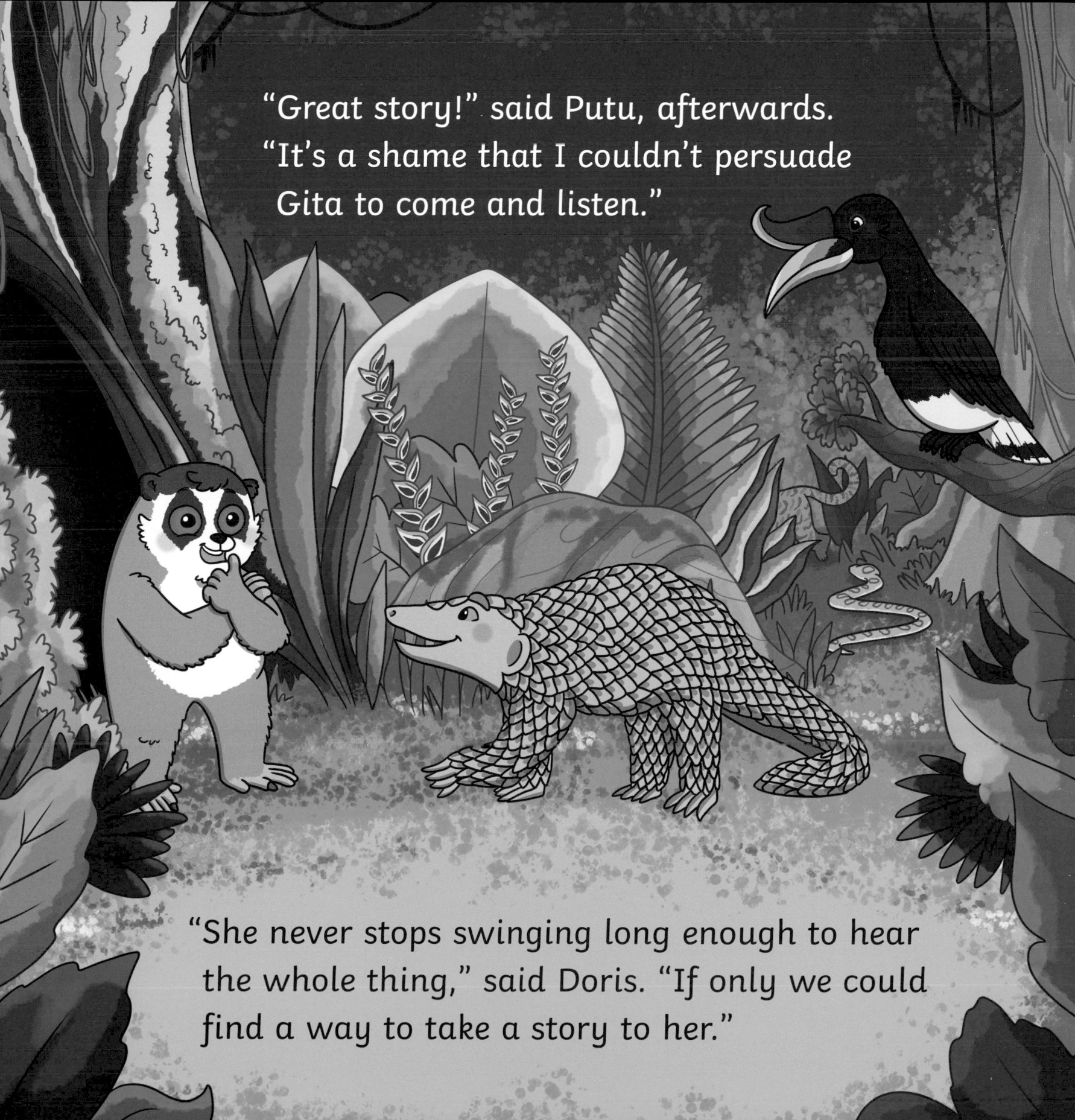

"Great story!" said Putu, afterwards. "It's a shame that I couldn't persuade Gita to come and listen."

"She never stops swinging long enough to hear the whole thing," said Doris. "If only we could find a way to take a story to her."

"It's funny you should say that!" squawked Harta the hornbill. "I wish that I could take your stories home to settle my babies at night. I can never remember the endings!"

They headed off on their way but an idea was forming in Doris's mind. She needed to find a way for her friends to take her stories with them wherever they went.

Early the next morning, Doris headed off to put her plan into action. She found a big green leaf on the forest floor.

'I wonder...' thought Doris.

Doris tried to make marks on the leaf using mud but it was too oozy.

She tried to sketch marks using a stick but the leaf kept tearing.

Then, Doris noticed some purple berries lying on the ground. A feather floated down from a nest above and she knew what to do.

Doris spent the rest of the day working hard to create her first three books.

To start with, she wrote an adventure story for Gita. It was about a gibbon setting a world record for swinging from the tallest tree.

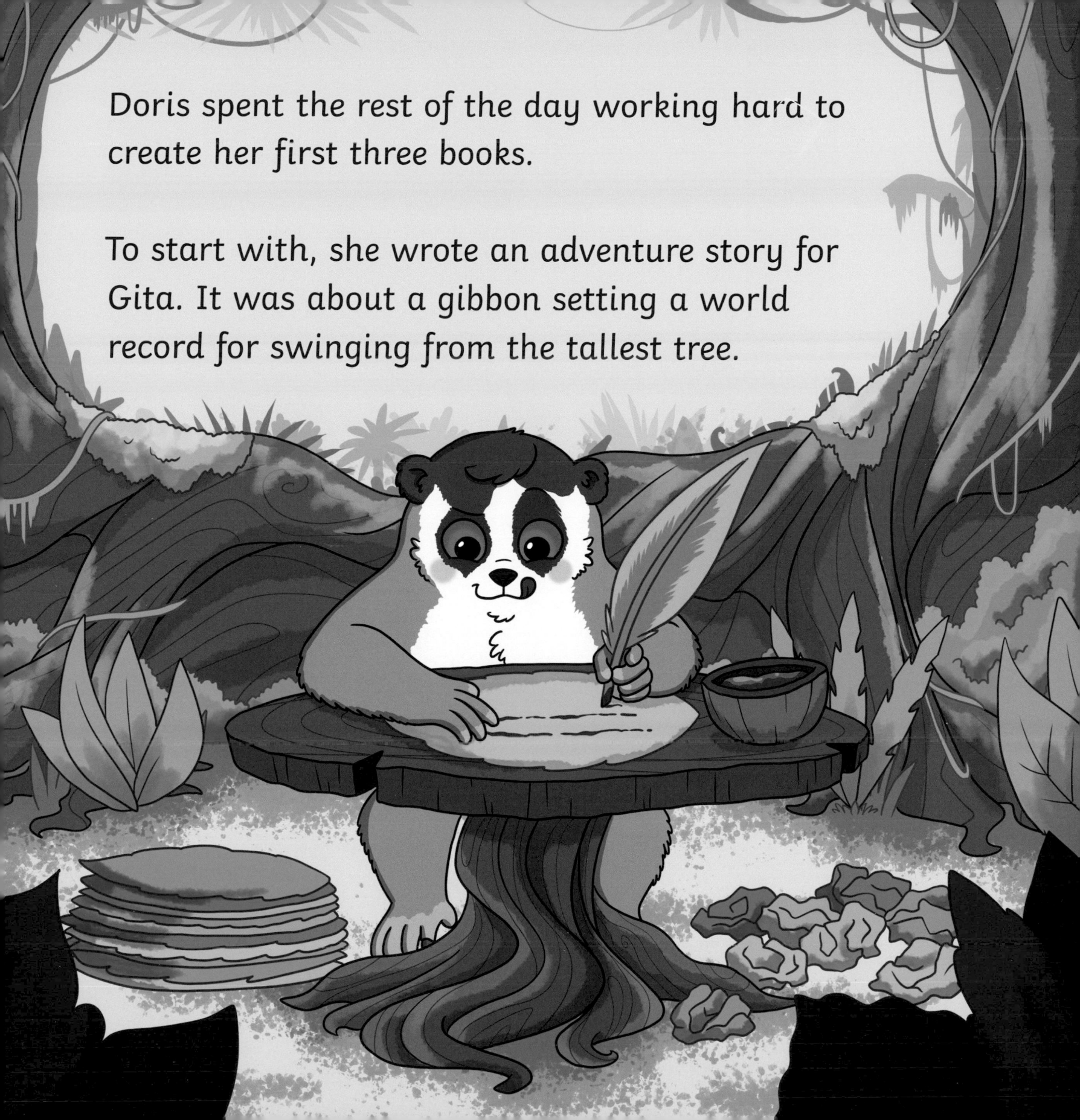

Next, she wrote a rhyming story about rhinos to give to the baby hornbills.

Finally, she wrote a non-fiction book about Putu's favourite tree – the rainbow eucalyptus.

Five
Cheeky
Rhinos

She delivered the books and hoped that their readers would be as excited as she was.

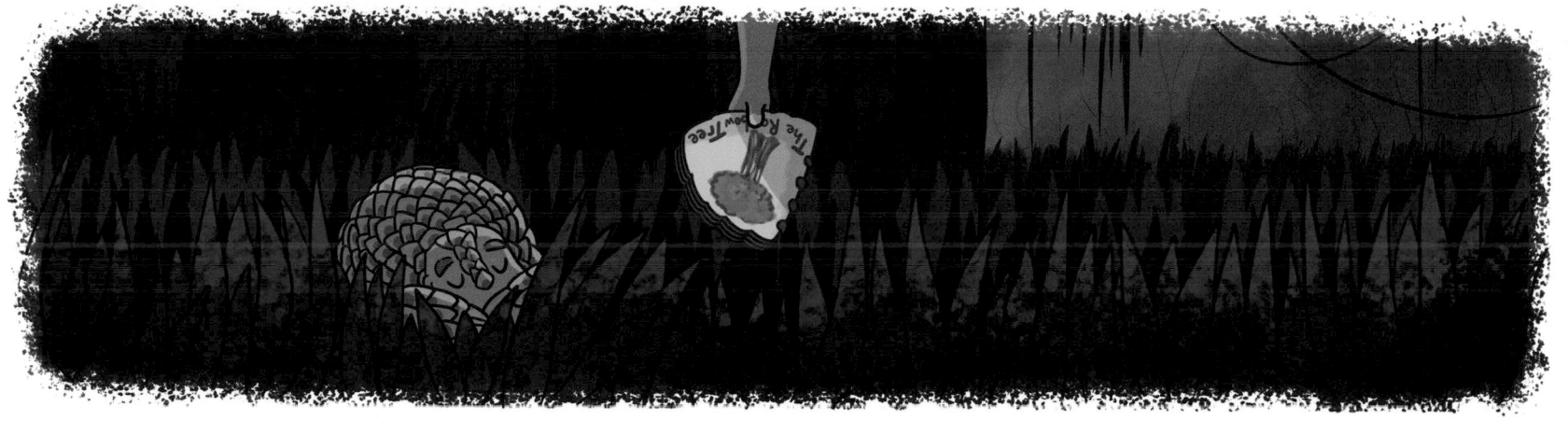

The next day, Doris had a surprise visitor.

"Putu was right," said Gita. "Your stories **aren't** boring! It's great being able to read them on the go. Do you have any more?"

Just then, Harta flew past. "Thank you for the story, Doris!" he shrieked. "My babies have never slept so well! Do you have any more?"

A smile began to creep across Doris's face.

No one saw Doris for days...

No storytime for a few days. Back soon!

...except for the glow-worms, whose light helped her to work through the night.

Then one evening, Cam's call floated across the rainforest again.

"Storytime!" called Putu, running towards Doris's tree with a host of other creatures. He was pleased to see that Gita was swinging along with them.

But Doris was nowhere to be seen.

Instead, there was a sign on the door.

Library
this way →

The creatures found Doris waiting for them all to arrive. And there, in the tree beside her, were hundreds and hundreds of...

...books!

Every story that Doris had ever told was captured on beautiful green leaves, along with some brand new ones!

"You can come and borrow them whenever you like!" said Doris. "Then, when you've finished, just bring them back for someone else to read."

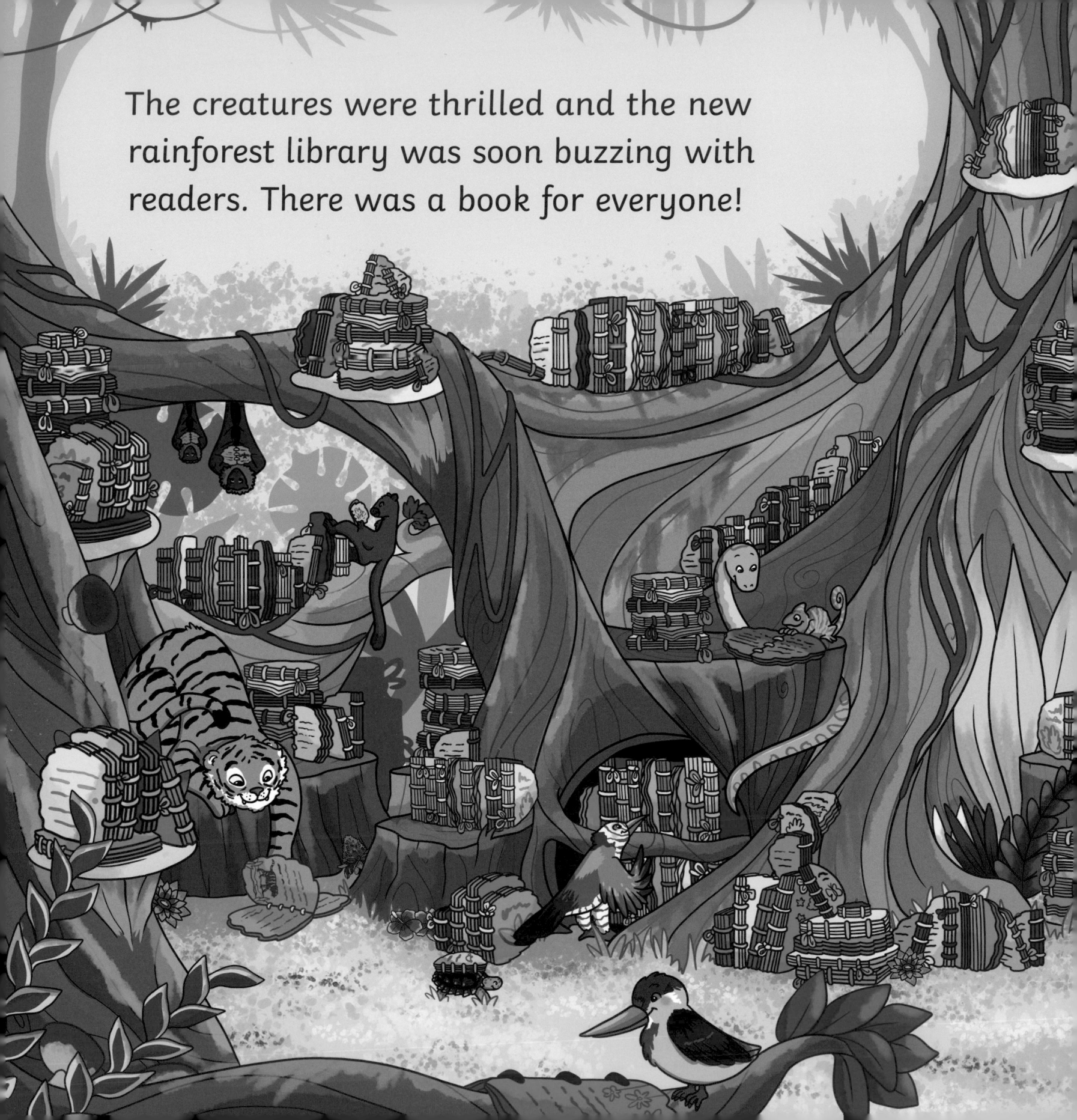

The creatures were thrilled and the new rainforest library was soon buzzing with readers. There was a book for everyone!

Doris became the first-ever rainforest author and librarian. She had found her dream job – bringing happiness to all of her friends every day, through the magic of reading.

Continue the learning with exclusive teacher-created resources to engage and inspire children at school, at home and beyond...

visit **twinkl.com/originals**

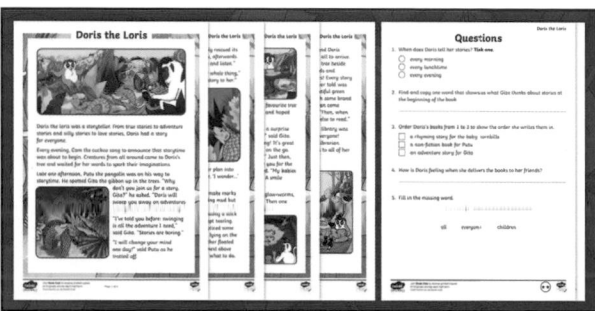

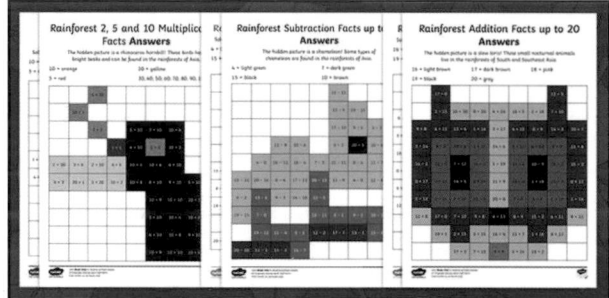

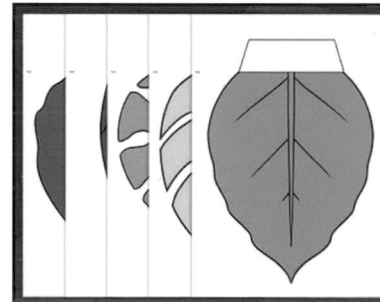

For accompanying teaching materials,
scan the QR code above or visit **twinkl.com/originals**